W9-BXV-596

Wombats

Barbara Triggs

Houghton Mifflin Company
Boston 1991

Stand quietly in the Australian bush in the late afternoon and, if you are very lucky, you might see a stocky, low-slung animal ambling along through the forest, grumbling softly to itself. Built like a mini-bulldozer, with a large broad head that swings slightly from side to side as it goes, this is the wombat, one of the world's largest burrowing mammals.

When Europeans came to settle in Australia 200 years ago, they soon began to explore. On one expedition in the Blue Mountains near Sydney the first settlers found a strange animal, which they thought was a kind of badger because it burrowed in the ground. The name the Aborigines gave this animal sounded like 'wombach' or 'womat', so it became known as a wombat.

A European badger

Although the badgers of Europe and the wombats of Australia both dig burrows in the ground, they are not related. Like many of Australia's remarkable mammals, the wombat is a marsupial. This means that the female protects and feeds her young in a pouch.

The wombat's pouch is on the mother's lower body wall, just like the kangaroo's pouch, but there is a difference. When a kangaroo is carrying a joey, her pouch expands mostly towards her flanks and rear, so that it forms a kind of pocket. A wombat's pouch expands in all directions, but mainly towards her chest, so that the opening faces towards the mother's tail.

A wombat's pouch opens backwards.

A kangaroo with a joey in her pouch

A koala

The koala is the wombat's closest relative. A female koala also has a backward-facing pouch.

There are two kinds of wombats. They are similar in many ways, but one has a soft leathery nose which is free of hair, while the other has a covering of fine white hairs all over its nose.

The nose is soft and leathery.

Fine white hairs cover the nose.

The bare-nosed wombats are called Common Wombats. They live in the cool, wet forests on the mountain ranges of south-eastern and southern Australia and in Tasmania. As their name suggests, they are fairly common, although their range is much smaller than it was 200 years ago because so many of these forests have been destroyed.

Distribution of Common Wombats

Areas where Common Wombats are found today

Areas where they were probably present before European settlement

Wombats are not found throughout the areas shaded [ ] but only where the habitat is suitable.

Common Wombat

Southern Hairy-nosed Wombat

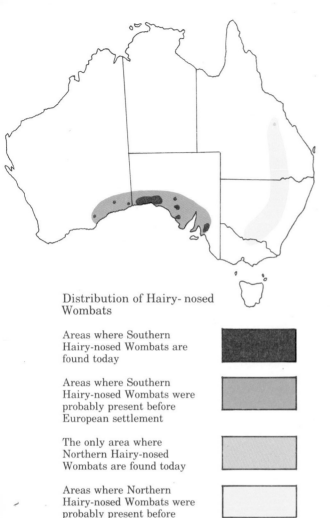

Distribution of Hairy- nosed Wombats

Areas where Southern Hairy-nosed Wombats are found today	
Areas where Southern Hairy-nosed Wombats were probably present before European settlement	
The only area where Northern Hairy-nosed Wombats are found today	
Areas where Northern Hairy-nosed Wombats were probably present before European settlement	

Northern Hairy-nosed Wombat

There are two groups of hairy-nosed wombats. Southern Hairy-nosed Wombats live on the dry grassland plains of South Australia and in a few small colonies on the Nullabor Plain in Western Australia. These wombats were much more widespread before European settlers began stocking the grasslands with sheep and cattle. Rabbits also competed with the wombats for food.

The Northern Hairy-nosed Wombats have been almost completely wiped out by the effects of introduced grazing animals such as sheep, cattle and rabbits. There are only about 70 of these wombats left. They live in a small colony in central Queensland and this area is now part of a national park which has been fenced so that cattle are kept out. Before the colony was protected, their numbers were as low as 30 or 40. They are still among the rarest mammals in the world.

This young wombat's small tail will be hidden by fur when it is older.

Wombats are sturdy, thickset animals, weighing two or even three times as much as a dog of about the same size. Their heads are broad and strong but their tails are small and short. The tail of the adult wombat is usually completely hidden by fur so that there often seems to be no tail at all!

A silky-furred hairy-nosed wombat

A Common Wombat's thick, coarse fur is usually grey or grey-brown, but it can be other colors as you can see in the photographs.

Hairy-nosed wombats are also usually grey or grey-brown but their fur is soft and silky and their ears are longer and more pointed than those of Common Wombats.

Front foot

With their short legs and powerful shoulders, wombats are well adapted for digging burrows. Their front paws have five strong, spade-like claws which they use to loosen the soil. Then the broad, padded palms scoop up the loose earth and push it out sideways and backwards.

The hind feet are longer and narrower. Only four of the toes on the hind foot have claws and these are also used to push and kick the soil out of the burrow. The inner toe looks like a small clawless thumb.

Hind foot

When a wombat is digging a burrow, it
first loosens the soil with its front paws . . .

. . . then scoops out the loose earth.

Backing away from the hole, the wombat
uses its hind feet to push the earth away
from the burrow.

If you are bushwalking in any of the places where wombats live, you might come across a large heap of earth and stones that looks as if it had been dumped. Look carefully and you will find the hole that is the entrance to the wombat's burrow.

The soil dug out of the burrow forms the large mound outside the entrance. If there are signs of fresh scratchings or footprints, a wombat is probably inside, lying asleep in a scooped-out chamber at the end of one of the tunnels. If it is a large, well-established burrow, the tunnels may be 30 meters (about 100 feet) or more in length.

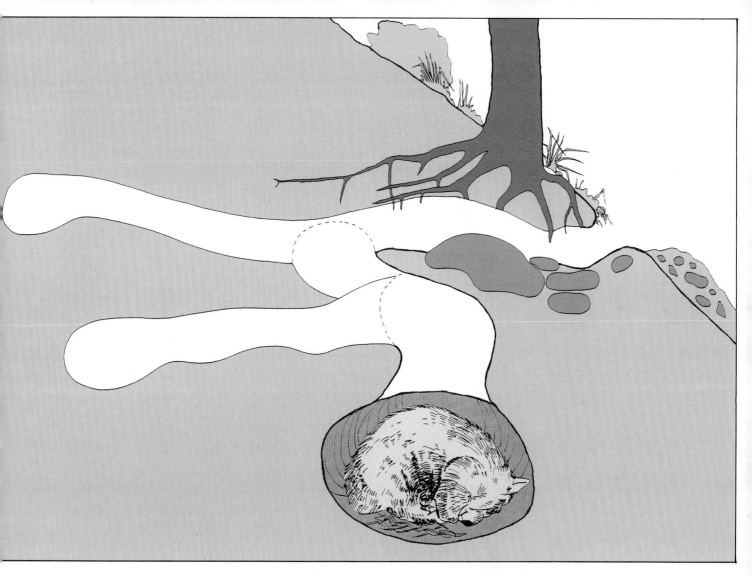

Cut-away diagram of a Common Wombat's burrow

It is very likely that the sleeping wombat is lying flat on its back, especially if the weather is hot. On cooler days it lies on its side, curled up in a ball.

The wombat is probably alone in the burrow, unless it is a mother with her young. If there is more than one adult in the burrow, they will sleep as far apart as possible. Wombats seem to like being on their own!

Burrow of the Southern Hairy-nosed Wombat on the Nullabor Plain

If the burrow belongs to a Southern Hairy-nosed Wombat, there will probably be a cluster of entrances nearby. These wombats often dig ten or more tunnels close together, forming warrens — like large-scale rabbit warrens. Many of the tunnels connect under the ground. Warrens are often dug under shelving limestone rocks which support the roofs of the tunnels. These might otherwise collapse in sandy soil.

Burrow of the Northern Hairy-nosed Wombat in an old river bed

Most of the burrows belonging to the Northern Hairy-nosed Wombats are also clustered in small groups. They are dug in deep river sand, as the area where these wombats live is the bed of a stream which dried up long ago. Most of the entrances are close to trees and the roots support the tunnel roofs.

A wombat sits at a burrow entrance.

Wombat scats

Common Wombats also have to dig their burrows in places where they will not collapse. They often dig under rocks and fallen trees or at the base of large trees so that the big roots give support to the tunnel roofs. The sloping hillsides above creeks and gullies are favored places for these burrows, which usually have only one entrance. Occasionally two or three burrows are dug close together with their tunnels connecting underground, but they do not form warrens like those of their hairy-nosed relatives.

A Common Wombat has a number of burrows, sometimes a dozen or more, scattered over its home range — the area where that particular wombat lives. A Common Wombat's home range can be as large as 25 hectares (about 60 acres), but will be smaller if there is plenty of grass and good burrow sites.

A wombat often shares part of its home range with other wombats, resting in the same burrows, though usually at different times.

Near a burrow you might find a wombat's scats — large, squarish-shaped droppings. These are also often found along roads and tracks in the bush. Sometimes they are piled on top of a stone or a fallen branch. Wombats use their scats to 'mark' their home range, leaving them as messages for other wombats.

Having a burrow as a shelter is very important for wombats. Because they are not good at keeping their body temperature at a constant level in hot weather, they become very distressed and can even die if they are exposed to temperatures over 35°C (95°F) for any length of time. Even in the hottest weather, the air in the burrow remains cool and humid.

Burrows also provide protection against the cold. In the mountains where many Common Wombats live, the ground is often snow-covered in winter. On the arid Nullabor Plain and in other places where hairy-nosed wombats live, winter temperatures often fall below freezing. Even in the coldest winter weather, temperatures in wombat burrows do not fall below 4°C (about 40°F).

Southern Hairy-nosed Wombat basking

Wombats often bask in the sun near their burrows, especially in winter.

Wombats do not leave their burrows until it is about as cool outside as it is in the burrow, so it is usually dusk or dark when they come out to feed. In very hot weather, they often stay in their burrows until early morning, when the temperature is at its lowest. In winter they sometimes come out to graze on cool, cloudy afternoons, especially after a night or two of bad weather.

'Muddle-headed', 'slow' and 'stupid' are words that have often been used to describe wombats. In fact, they are none of these. A wombat's brain is large and well developed — much more developed than that of the koala. With a very acute sense of smell and excellent hearing, a wombat is not nearly as placid as it might look! At the first hint or crackle of danger, the wombat is alert and running for the safety of the burrow.

Wombats can run as fast as 40 km/hour (nearly 25 mph) over short distances if they have to, but they usually move about at a slow amble. They give the impression of being lazy because the best way for them to survive is to take life slowly and easily, conserving their energy in as many ways as possible. Their bodies are adapted to a very economical way of living. Because they use up energy at a slow rate, they need less food than other animals of similar size. This means they do not have to eat for more than a few hours each night.

A Common Wombat leaves the burrow at dusk.

By saving energy, wombats also reduce the amount of water lost from their bodies. This is particularly important for the hairy-nosed wombats who live where there is very little rain. These wombats do not drink, but get most of the water they need from the plants they eat and the dew which has fallen on the plants. They also save energy by grazing as close to their burrows as possible, rarely going more than about 700 meters (about half a mile) from their warrens in search of food.

All animals lose water from their bodies in their urine and faeces (scats). Wombats conserve water by producing only very small amounts of urine and their scats are among the driest known for any mammal.

If you come across a wombat feeding, the chances are that it is eating one of the coarse native grasses. Common Wombats particulary like kangaroo grass, spear grass and tussock grass, but also eat rushes and sedges. They even eat sword grass, in spite of its razor-sharp leaves! Digging is no problem to wombats, so when the ground is covered in snow they simply scoop the snow away to reach their food. Hairy-nosed wombats also like spear grass but sometimes, during severe droughts, they have to eat the scrubby bushes such as bluebush and bindyi.

To get as much nutriment from their tough, high-fiber food as possible, wombats grind it up very thoroughly. Their teeth are specially designed to cope with this. They are rootless and grow continuously, so they are not worn away by the constant grinding.

The wombat's digestive system is also very efficient. In order to extract nourishment and water from the coarse, often very dry grass, the food passes slowly through the colon, or large intestine, sometimes taking as long as 3 days.

Wombat rubbing its rump on a tree stump

Wombats keep themselves remarkably clean, considering that their underground homes are usually dusty and sometimes even muddy.

They do not lick their fur clean as most mammals do, but scratch themselves often and thoroughly. They are able to reach most parts of their bodies with either their front or back paws. They also rub themselves against tree trunks and other convenient rubbing posts, relieving some of the itchy places their paws cannot reach.

Sometimes a wombat will lie on a patch of sandy or dusty ground and have a dust-bath, scooping up the loose sand or soil with a front paw and flinging it over its body. You might see hollows on beaches or sandy tracks where wombats have been dust-bathing.

Wombat having a dust-bath

Wombats are mature enough to breed by their third or fourth year. Because it is important that there is plenty of green grass for the mother to eat while she is providing her baby with milk, she will usually wait until seasonal conditions are good before she begins her reproductive cycle.

During this cycle the female wombat produces an egg, or ovum, in her reproductive system in the process called ovulation. A little while before ovulation, special glands release scented substances, called pheromones, in a secretion released with the wombat's urine and scats. This scent attracts male wombats and lets them know that the female is nearly ready to mate. If, during mating, the ovum is fertilized by a sperm from a male wombat, it will stay in the mother's womb, or uterus, and begin to develop into an embryo.

As the time for mating approaches, there is much activity at the warrens and burrows. Tunnels are cleaned out and lots of fresh soil is scratched out on to the mounds. Normally fairly peaceful animals, male wombats will fight each other around mating time, biting and lunging and often giving and receiving quite severe wounds. The females fight the males, too, until they are ready to mate. Most adult wombats have torn ears or scarred faces.

Mating takes place when the male, having chased the female into her burrow, manages to force her to roll on to her side, clasping her with his front paws. After mating, the female chases the male away. He does not look after his mate or help her to care for the young in any way at all.

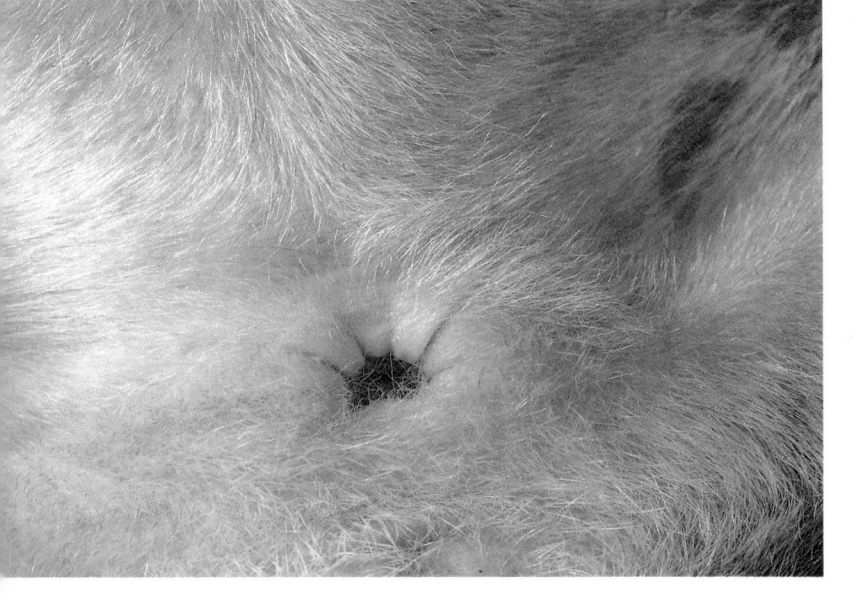

The opening to the pouch

so that the inside of the pouch is kept warm, moist and clean.

The baby wombat stays attached to the same teat for more than 3 months, sucking its mother's milk and growing slowly but steadily. Its eyes open when it is about 4 months old and about a month later its fur begins to appear. Although it is no longer permanently attached to the teat, it still suckles frequently, lying on its back much of the time, swinging comfortably in the pouch.

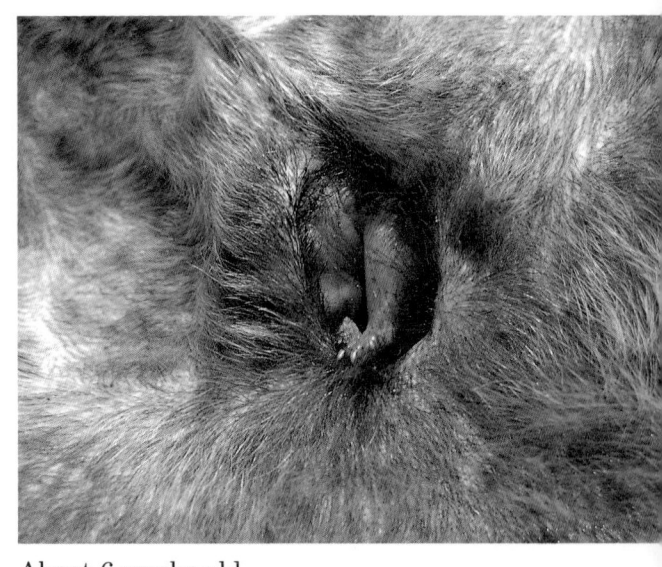

About 6 weeks old

About 3 or 4 weeks after mating the young wombat is born. Because it has been in the mother's uterus for such a short time, it is still very undeveloped and only about the size of a small bean. The tiny, pink newborn wombat emerges from the birth canal and uses its front legs and sharp, curved claws to grasp the mother's fur and haul its way to her pouch, which is lined with soft, moist skin. There are two teats inside the pouch and the embryo-like wombat fastens on to one of them. The teat then swells inside the mouth so that the young wombat is firmly attached. A strong circular muscle closes the pouch opening,

The front teeth break through the gums at 6 months and the young wombat occasionally pokes its head out of the pouch and nibbles grass.

As the baby grows the pouch stretches, but by the time the young wombat is 7 months old it is so big that the pouch sometimes drags on the ground.

By then, the baby has a thicker coat of fur and will venture out of the pouch when the mother is in the burrow, but quickly scrambles back if she makes a

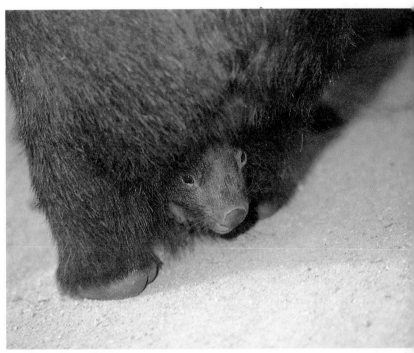

About 6 months old

About 3 months old

move to leave. The soles of the baby wombat's feet are soft and pink. There is much walking and digging to be done before they become dark and leathery!

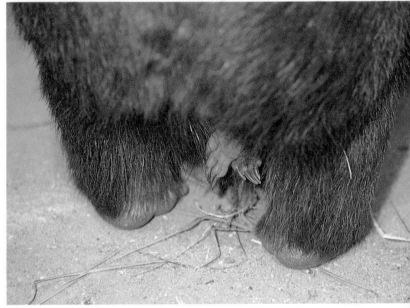

The baby whose feet are visible at the entrance of the pouch is about 6 months old.

Over the next 2 or 3 months the young wombat spends more and more time out of the pouch. It still suckles from the teat, but also eats increasing amounts of grass. It stays close to its mother at all times and she will protect it fiercely if danger threatens. If they are separated, as sometimes happens when they are alarmed and have to run for the shelter of a burrow, the young wombat will make a 'huh huh' sound, or, if very frightened, will give a sharp, high-pitched cough. The mother will call her young one with the soft 'huh huh' sound or a sharper cough when there is danger.

A young wombat is as playful as a puppy. It will race around its
mother, toss its head from side to side, roll over onto its side, then
jump into the air before racing off again. It will run up a slope and
roll down, tumbling over and over. Sometimes it will pounce on its
mother in a mock battle, or climb onto her back, grabbing mouthfuls
of her fur and butting her with its forehead.

By 10 months, the young wombat is ready to leave the pouch permanently, though until at least 12 months and sometimes as much as 15 months of age it still pushes its head inside to suckle from the teat. Some young wombats leave their mother soon after weaning, but others stay with her until they are nearly as big as she is!

Weaning and the first few months of independence are risky times for the young wombat. It is important that there is a good supply of fresh green grass, as the wombat is growing fast and it can no longer rely on its mother's milk supply. If the rains fail in autumn, many young hairy-nosed wombats die in late winter and spring as they cannot cope with a diet of dry, rank grass left from the previous summer. Common Wombats also suffer during years of drought.

A mother wombat will fight to protect her young, even when it is as big as this one!

Others hazards face young wombats. Dingoes, feral dogs (domestic dogs gone wild) and foxes all hunt and often kill wombats, especially young ones and older, weaker animals.

Although a healthy adult wombat might be able to defend itself against a single dingo or dog, these predators often hunt in packs or family groups and a wombat out in the open has no chance of fighting them off. If it can reach a burrow and block the entrance with its broad rump, the wombat can save itself by squeezing its enemy's head against the roof of the tunnel.

The burrow is also a refuge against the bushfires that rage through the forests and grasslands of Australia in the summer. Wombats can stay relatively cool and safe deep inside their burrows during a fire, though when a large area is burnt in a severe fire, many die from lack of food after the fire.

By far the worst dangers facing wombats are caused by humans. Although now protected by law, they are sometimes still treated as pests, mainly because of their habit of burrowing under fences and making holes in wire-netting. Rabbit-proof fences stop being rabbit-proof when a wombat has passed through or under them! Some farmers use electric fences to stop this damage and others have installed swinging 'wombat gates' which are too heavy for rabbits to push but are no problem to the sturdy wombats.

Every year, thousands of wombats are hit by cars and trucks on the roads. A motorist who stops to look often finds that, although the wombat is dead, it is a female with a young one in the pouch, still alive. These orphan wombats, if cared for by experienced people, can be hand-reared, and when they are old enough they can be released back into the wild.

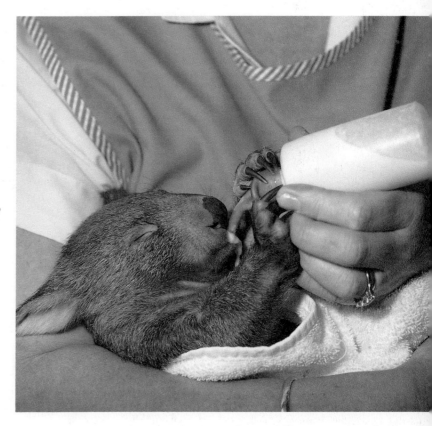

There they can dig and scratch, amble and grumble, and maybe, some day, have young of their own.

Library of Congress Cataloging-in-Publication Data:

Triggs, Barbara
    Wombats/Barbara Triggs. – 1st American ed.
        p.   cm.
    Summary: Presents, in text and photographs, the habits, life
cycle and natural environment of the Australian Wombat, one of the
world's largest burrowing animals.
    ISBN 0-395-55993-6
    1. Wombats – Juvenile literature. [1. Wombats.] I. Title.
    QL737.M39T75 1991   90-34042
    599.2—dc20   CIP
                                                   AC

Printed in Hong Kong by South China Printing Company Limited.

10 9 8 7 6 5 4 3 2 1

ACKNOWLEDGEMENTS
Much of the material in this book is based on research carried out by Dr John McIlroy, Dr Graham
Brown, Dr Rod Wells, Dr Doug Crossman, Dr Chris Johnson, Barbara St John and Gary Saunders.
Chris Johnson also assisted with further information and I thank him for his comments on an
earlier draft.

Photo credits
Grateful acknowledgement is made to the following photographers: Auscape International: cover,
pages 3, 9, 10 and 38 Jean-Paul Ferrero, 5 (left) and 7 John Cancalosi, 20 Mark Newton, 24 (left)
Gunther Deichmann, 37 Esther Beaton, 30 D. Parer and E. Parer-Cook; A.N.T. Photo Library:
pages 4 N.H.P.A., 6 (left) C. and S. Pollitt, 6 (right) D. and V. Blagden, 13 Natfoto, 18 Ford Kristo,
27 Bill Bachman, 34 and 35 Dave Watts; Ballarat Wildlife Park Images: pages 5 (right), 14, 15, 16
(both), 17, 22 (left), 28 (both right), 29 and 33 (both right) Greg Parker; Larus: pages 11 and 21
C. Andrew Henley; Kathie Atkinson: pages 12, 23, 28 (top left), 32 (left) and 39; Nevil Amos: page
24 (right); Peter Canty: page 25; Vi Merrett page 31; Joe Stelmann: page 32 (right); Barbara St
John: page 33 (left). Unacknowledged photographs are by the author.